Postman Pat's
Story Treasury

First published in Great Britain 2008 by Dean,
an imprint of Egmont UK Limited
239 Kensington High Street,
London W8 6SA

ISBN 978 0 6035 6368 3
1 3 5 7 9 10 8 6 4 2
Printed in Italy

Contents

5   Postman Pat the Hilltop Hero

15   Postman Pat and the Greendale Knights

25   Postman Pat and the Go-Kart Race

35   Postman Pat's Pet Rescue

43   Postman Pat's Hedgehog Hideaway

53   Postman Pat's Noisy Day

63   Postman Pat and the Cat Calamity

73   Postman Pat's Christmas Eve

Postman Pat the Hilltop Hero

One morning, Pat had a job to do before he went to work. He climbed a ladder to get rid of the leaves that were blocking the gutter on the roof.

"Thanks, Pat," said Sara. "I know you don't like heights."

Later on, Pat took some post to Thompson Ground.

Bill was helping his dad herd some sheep into the trailer.

"We're moving them up to the hills near Greendale Crag," said Alf. "There's more grass for them there."

Bill patted his pet sheep, Bessie. "I wish Bessie could stay on the farm," he said.

Bessie agreed!

"Baaaaaa!"

Pat gave Bill a lift to the railway station where Julian, Meera and Sara were waiting. Ajay was taking them all on a walk to Greendale Crag.

Ajay followed his map. "This way," he said. "Through this gate and across the field."

Ajay closed the gate carefully, but it swung open again!

Alf had put his sheep in the next field. Bessie and another sheep ran out through the gate. They wanted to go back to the farm!

Pat was driving back to
Greendale when he saw the
sheep on the edge of the
crag. "That's Bessie!" he said.
"She shouldn't be up here!"
Pat tried to move the
sheep away from the cliff. But Bessie was scared and she ran off
down a steep path. She got stuck on a tiny ledge!
Ajay and the children were sitting around a camp fire at the

bottom of the crag when
Bill heard, **"Baaaaaa!"**
"That's Bessie!" he said.
Pat went to the edge
of the cliff and
shouted down.
Bessie's stuck!"
he said. "Get
help, Ajay!"

Ajay found Amy in her jeep and told her about Bessie.

Amy drove to the top of the crag. She put on a harness and tied her climbing rope to a tree.

"Ready!" said Amy, and she swung out over the edge of the cliff. Down she went,

down . . .

down . . .

down.

When she got to the ledge, Amy put a harness on Bessie.

"Baaa, baaa!" said Bessie. She was very pleased to see her.

But when Amy started to climb down, the rope got stuck on a rock. Amy and Bessie swayed around in mid-air!

"You'll have to climb down and free it, Pat!" said Amy.

Pat gulped. "Erm ... all right," he said. "Hold on, I'm coming!"

Pat put on a harness and tied a rope around the tree.

Then he took a big, deep breath — and stepped over the edge of the cliff!

Down he went, down ...

down ...

down.

Bill and the others watched from the bottom of the crag.

"Your dad's really brave, Julian," said Bill.

"I know," said Julian. "And he's scared of heights!"

Pat pulled Amy's rope free and she climbed down with Bessie.

Bill was so pleased to see her that he gave her a big hug.

Bessie was pleased to see Bill, too. **"Baaa, baaa, baaa!"** she bleated.

When Pat climbed down, Julian gave him an extra big hug.
"I thought you were afraid of heights, Dad," he said. "I am,"
said Pat. "But I had to rescue Amy and Bessie, didn't I?"
Bill clapped and the others joined in. "Three cheers for Pat!"
he said. "What a hero!"

Postman Pat and the Greendale Knights

One morning, Mrs Goggins had some parcels for Pat.
"They're plants," said Pat. "Sara's going out for the day, so I'm tidying up the garden as a surprise for her."

At Forge Cottage, Julian, Bill, Lucy and Meera were playing a game of knights.

Julian knelt down. "I knight you Sir Julian, Knight of Greendale," said Bill, proudly.

"Can I be a knight?" asked Meera.

"No," said Bill. "Girls can't be knights."

"Oh, yeah?" said Meera.

"Yeah," said Bill. "They have to fight dragons and stuff. They have to be strong."

When Pat got home, he took some of the parcels out of his van.

Lucy wanted to help. She grabbed a big parcel, but it was much too heavy for her.

"I told you, girls can't be knights," said Bill. "You're not strong enough."

"Oh, yes we are!" said Meera.

She grabbed a parcel. Meera wanted to show how strong she was.

So did Bill! But they both tripped and fell over!

"You'd better leave the parcels to me," said Pat.

"OK, Dad," said Julian. "Come on, we'll look for dragons!"

"D-d-d-dragons?" said Lucy.

"See, girls are scared of everything," said Bill.

"Well I'm not!" said Meera.

Just then, Lucy heard a loud noise. It made her jump.

"It's a d-d-dragon!" she said.

"It's Dad's tractor," said Bill. "Only a girl would be scared of a tractor!"

Alf unloaded the arbour he had brought for Pat.

"You make it into an arch shape, plant roses around it, and they grow up the sides," Pat explained.

Then Pat dug a new flower bed.

The empty compost bags gave him an idea! He cut neck and armholes in one, and put it on Julian.

"There you are," he said. "Armour!"

Pat made armour for the others. Then he made visors and shields from the plant boxes. Wooden spoons made good swords!

"Now we can fight like real knights!" said Julian.

"Take that!" said Meera.

"Take that!" said Bill.

"Oh, please stop," said Lucy.

"I don't like fighting!" Julian
had no one to fight with!

"Maybe Bill's right," he said.

"Girls can't be knights."

Meera and Bill got a bit carried away! "Look out!" said Pat.

Too late! They crashed into the arbour and knocked it flat.

"I think that's enough fighting," said Pat. "Go and have a drink to cool down."

There was a big surprise waiting for the Greendale Knights when they went back into the garden. Pat had made a castle out of the plant boxes.

Bill, Meera and Julian went inside. They left Lucy outside to guard the castle.

When Lucy saw smoke coming from behind the house she told the others.

"Is it a dragon?" asked Meera.

"No, it's a scary knight!" said Bill.

"Look, he's got a fire sword!"

"Hide!" said Julian.

Poor Lucy was on her own. She wanted to hide, but she was on guard. "I have to protect the castle," she said. "I must be brave."

She picked up the water hose, turned it on, and fired it at the knight.

But it wasn't a knight, it was Ted! He had come to fix the arbour with his blow torch! Splash! He was drenched!

The knights came out of the castle.

"You saved us, Lucy," said Julian.

"Yes, you were really brave," said Bill.

Julian asked Pat to knight Lucy. He touched her shoulders with a wooden spoon. "I knight you Lady Lucy Selby," he said.

The knights helped Pat to finish the garden.

When Sara came home she could hardly believe her eyes! "Oh, it's lovely," she said. "Thank you, Pat!"

"Don't thank me," said Pat. "Thank the Greendale Knights!"

Postman Pat and the Go-Kart Race

Mrs Goggins told everyone about the Greendale go-kart race. She explained the rules. "You must make your own go-kart. You can push, pull or pedal it. But you can't use an engine."

Pat, PC Selby, Ajay and Alf got busy making their karts. But things didn't go too well!

First, Pat's kart rattled, shook, then fell apart . . .

PC Selby hit his thumb with a hammer . . .

Ajay ended up head-first in his Greendale Rocket-kart . . .

Alf's tractor-kart zoomed off down a hill!

PC Selby went to see Ted. "Can I borrow an electric engine?" he asked. "It's for . . . er . . . police business."

"All right," said Ted. "But remember, the engine won't . . ." But PC Selby had gone.

Ajay borrowed an engine, and so did Alf. They didn't listen to Ted either.

Pat made a wind sail for his kart. "When the wind blows it goes really fast," he said. But the kart went so fast that it crashed and ended up in pieces!

Later that day, Julian met up with Meera, Bill and Lucy.

"My dad's really bad at making go-karts," said Meera.

"So's mine," said Julian.

"Mine won't even let me help," said Bill.

"Let's make our own go-kart," said Lucy. "A kids'-kart."

"Yes!" said Julian. "We'll use what's left of Dad's kart. It's in bits, but it just needs . . . um . . . a bit of work."

On the day of the race all the go-karts lined up.

Jeff said, "Everybody ready?"

"Ready!" said Ajay, in his green rocket-kart.

"Ready!" said Alf, in his red tractor-kart.

"Ready!" said PC Selby, in his blue police-car-kart.

"Ready!" said Julian, in his pedal-kart.

"On your marks, get set … **go!**" said Jeff.

Ajay, Alf and PC Selby switched on the engines of their karts and zoomed off. Julian pedalled as fast as he could, but his kart was soon left behind.

"Does Julian's kart have an engine?" Ted asked Pat.

"Oh, no," said Pat. "That's against the rules. There are no engines allowed."

"Oh …" said Ted.

The go-karts zoomed around the village. First Alf was in the lead. Then Ajay. Then PC Selby. Poor Julian

was so slow that they all passed him on their second lap.

Minutes later Ajay, PC Selby and Alf sped past the finishing line. Jeff waved his flag, but they didn't stop.

"What's happening?" asked Pat.

"They wouldn't listen when I warned them about the engines," said Ted.

"They switch ON, but they won't switch OFF!"

PC Selby, Alf and Ajay moved the STOP switch backwards and forwards, but the karts didn't stop. They sped out of the village on the road to Greendale Crag!

When Julian's pedal-kart got to the finishing line for the first time, Pat got in. He fitted the wind sail and they set off after the runaway karts.

The wind-kart sped along, and Pat and Julian watched as Ajay flew into a bush ...

Alf crashed into a bale of hay ...

and PC Selby landed in a pile of manure!

"Urrgh!" said Pat.

"What a pong!" said Julian.

Later on, Jeff announced the result of the race. "Alf, Ajay and PC Selby cheated by using engines," he said. "So the winners of the Greendale go-kart race are — Julian, Meera, Bill and Lucy!"

Everyone clapped and cheered: **"Hip, hip, hooray!"**

Postman Pat's Pet Rescue

When Julian came down for breakfast one morning, he sneezed: "Atishoo! Atishoo!"

"You've got a cold," said Pat. "Stay at home today and I'll look after you. Mrs Goggins will deliver the post for me."

Pat took Julian back to bed.

"Can't I sit on the sofa and watch television?" asked Julian.

"No," said Pat. "Stay in bed. If you need anything, just ring this little bell and I'll come up."

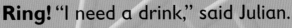

Naughty Julian wasn't really very ill. He thought a day off school would be fun, but it wasn't! "Oh, this is so b-o-r-i-n-g," he said.

Ring! Julian rang the bell. When Pat came in he said, "Could you bring me my comic book, please, Dad?"

Ring! "I need a drink," said Julian.

Ring! "Can I have my superhero toy?"

Ring! "Will you bring my truck?"

Julian kept Pat busy all morning.

Pat and Julian didn't have any time for Jess, so Jess went off into the village. He met Bonnie there, and they ran off to an old well.

Woof!" said Bonnie. Meow!" said Jess.

They ran round and round, faster and faster. But when Jess stopped and looked over the edge, he fell in! **"Meoooooow!"** howled Jess. He was stuck, and his paw hurt.

Bonnie looked into the well. "Woof!" she barked, and ran off to get help.

Bonnie found Mrs Goggins. "Woof!" she barked, but Mrs Goggins didn't know what she wanted.

So Bonnie ran off to find Amy. "Woof!" she barked, tugging at Amy's trousers. "Woof!" Amy understood! "You want me to follow you!" she said. **"Woof!"** barked Bonnie, and she led Amy to the well.

Amy used ropes to climb down inside. She put Jess in a rescue cage and climbed out with him. Then she took Jess to the animal clinic and x-rayed his paw. It was broken!

Later, Sara had just come home from work when Amy rang to tell her about Jess.

"He fell down a hole and broke his leg," Sara told Pat and Julian. "Amy's looking after him at the clinic."

"Dad, it's my fault," said Julian. "If you hadn't been looking after me, Jess wouldn't have gone off, and he'd be OK ..."

"You can't help being ill," said Pat.

"But I'm not really ill," said Julian. "I was a bit sniffly at first, but then I pretended."

"Hmm," said Pat. "I see."

Pat, Sara and Julian went to collect Jess.

"Thanks for looking after him, Amy," said Pat. "Atishoo!
Atishoo!" Pat had caught
Julian's cold!

When he got home it
was his turn to stay in bed.
Ring, ring! Now it was
Julian's turn to look after
his dad!

Postman Pat's
Hedgehog Hideaway

Sara was going away for the night. Pat and Julian went to the station to say goodbye.

"Bye!" said Sara. "Don't forget your packed lunch, Julian."

"Don't worry, Mum," said Julian. "We won't forget anything."

But Pat had already forgotten something – his keys! When they got home they couldn't get in!

"Meow!" said Jess. He jumped in through a window. Julian followed him and opened the door for Pat. Julian made a peanut butter sandwich and put it in his lunch box.

"We're late," said Pat. "I'll drop you at school on my way to work."

When Pat got to the Post Office, he laughed. Mrs Goggins' dog, Bonnie, was sitting on the scales!

"Are you going to post her?" asked Pat.

"No," said Mrs Goggins. "I'm weighing her. She's always hungry, but she's losing weight."

"That's not good," said Pat.

He took Mrs Goggins and Bonnie to see Amy, the vet.

"All her food was gone this morning," Mrs Goggins told Amy. "But she wanted more."

"Give her some more food when you get home," said Amy. "I'll call in later to see how she is."

Pat delivered the post.
When he got back to the
Post Office, he went to
check on Bonnie.

She was in the
garden – and so was a
hedgehog. It was
eating her food!

"Woof, woof!" said Bonnie.
"So that's why she's always
hungry!" said Mrs Goggins.
"The hedgehog's been
eating her food!"

The hedgehog
scurried away.

"I'll catch it and
take it into the
countryside," said Pat.
He put some of
Bonnie's food into a
cardboard box and
propped it open with a stick.

After a while, the hedgehog
went into the box and Pat
pulled a string on the stick.
It fell away and the flap closed.
"Got him!" said Pat.

When Amy arrived, they took the hedgehog out into the countryside in her jeep.

That night, everything was quiet. The only sound that could be heard was snuffle-snuffle-snuffle! The hedgehog was going back to Greendale!

In the morning, Julian went to work with Pat. There was a surprise waiting for them. The hedgehog was back – with three babies! "The he is a she!" said Pat. "The mummy hedgehog came back for her babies."

Pat and Julian built a house to keep them safe.

The hedgehog family sniffled and snuffled, then they went inside.

"They like it!" said Julian.

"That's grand," said Mrs Goggins. "The hedgehogs have a lovely house and now Bonnie can eat her food in peace."

"**Woof!**" said Bonnie.

"**Meow!**" said Jess.

Pat laughed. "Now Bonnie only has to share it with Jess!"

Postman Pat's Noisy Day

It was the school holidays in Greendale. Pat asked Julian to help out for the day, he thought it might keep him out of trouble. When they arrived at the Post Office there were parcels everywhere!

"Looks like it's going to be a busy day, Pat." said Mrs Goggins.

"Good job I have a helping hand!" said Pat.

First stop was the Station Café, Meera was also looking bored. Pat handed the post to Nisha, "Morning!" he said.

"Thank you, Pat!" said Nisha, "Perhaps Julian can stay and keep Meera out of trouble."

"Thanks, Nisha" said Pat.

"Pat, could you pass me the coffee beans from the shelf?" Nisha asked as she wiped the counter.

Pat shook the jar as he handed it to Nisha, it made a rattling sound, "What a great noise!" said Pat.

Pat's next delivery was for Jeff, but it looked like no one was there. Pat could hear a swishing sound.

"Wait a minute, what's that noise?" said Pat.

Jeff and Charlie were in the garden. "I didn't think anyone was here until I heard the broom!" said Pat.

"Oh dear!" said Pat, "Looks like Charlie is bored too."

"Why don't you go and play with Julian and Meera at the Station Café?" said Pat.

"Hurrah!" cried Charlie as he hurried away.

When Charlie met Julian and Meera, they were playing target practice. When it came to Charlie's turn, he threw the ball hard . . . BANG! It hit PC Selby.

"Sorry!" said Charlie.

"You should be more careful!" said PC Selby, "Try to stay out of trouble."

All three children were embarrassed and looked at the ground.

When Pat arrived at
Greendale Farm, he heard a
strange whistling noise.
Katy and Tom were helping
their mum to make bread.
"Hello, Pat!" They chorused.
"What's that strange noise?"
asked Pat.

Then, he spotted Tom blowing into the top
of a bottle.
"Watch out, Katy!" cried Pat, as she spilt a bowl of flour.

"What a mess!"
said Pat. The twins
helped their mum
to clear away the
mess, as Pat left to
carry on with
his rounds.

When Pat arrived at the workshop, Ted Glen was sanding a wooden chair. It made a loud scratching noise, Pat could hear the sanding before he even walked through the door.

"What a great sound!" said Pat as he handed Ted a parcel.

"Thanks Pat, I was wondering when that would turn up," said Ted.

Pat's next stop was at the stables. He could see Amy and Sarah standing outside.

"Those are horse shoes, they are for Pumpkin's feet, not for banging together." Amy told Sarah.

"But they do make a good clanging noise!" Pat said as he climbed out of the van and handed the post to Amy.

"AH HA! I have had an idea! Could I borrow those horse shoes?" Pat asked.

" Of course, Pat" Amy replied. "Come to the school at tea time and all will be revealed!"

he said as he got back into the van. Pat drove by the children, "Meet me at the school room in an hour! I've had an idea!" he cried.

Along the way, Pat stopped to make some rather unusual collections. He picked up a coffee jar from the Station Café, a broom from Jeff, a whistle from PC Selby and some sanding blocks from Ted.

When Pat arrived everyone was waiting in the school room.

"What's all this about Pat?" asked Bill.

"As you have all been making a lot of noise, I thought you could put on a concert for everyone," said Pat.

"But where are our instruments?" Katy asked, looking puzzled.

"We are going to try something different!" said Pat, as he started to rub the sanding blocks together. "Can you hear that noise?" Pat asked the children. They all nodded and began looking at all the objects Pat had gathered together. "Brilliant!" said Tom.

Pat handed out the items to the children, and showed them how they could use them to make lots of noises. Soon everybody had gathered in the school room to watch the concert. One by one the children started to play, with Pat conducting them.

When the concert had finished, there was a large round of applause even Jess gave a loud MEOW! "Oh, well done Pat! Who would've thought making noise could be so much fun!" said Tom and Katy's mum. Everybody cheered in agreement.

Postman Pat and the Cat Calamity

One afternoon, the children of Greendale were playing in the tree house.

"Come on everybody, let's play spaceships! I will be the Mission Commander!" said Sarah.

"Bossy or what?" said Bill.

"Ready for blast off? Five, four, three, two …" Sarah cried. Bill was annoyed.

Sarah started to climb down from the tree house, "It's my game, I am the Mission Commander and I want to do the countdown! You can play on your own!" exclaimed Sarah, huffily.

"We will! You're too bossy anyway …" said Bill.

"Let's play hunting for aliens," Julian said. They all laughed as Sarah walked away.

Meanwhile, PC Selby found Ted Glen standing outside his
house. The ground was covered in litter.

"The bins should have been emptied weeks ago," said PC Selby.
"When it's windy the village is covered in litter."

Ted thought for a moment.

"Hold on, I think I've got something that will help …"

Ted came back with a strange-looking machine.

"What on earth is that?" asked PC Selby.

"It's the Ted Glen Automatic Litter Blower! I made it myself
out of a vacuum cleaner, watch this," said Ted, as he flew into the
air and began to blow the litter into piles.

As Pat left the Post Office, a piece of litter blew up into his face. Pat noticed Sarah sitting by herself.

"Oh, hello Sarah, is something wrong?" Pat asked.

"The others say I am bossy, but I have all the ideas. Now they won't play with me!" grumbled Sarah.

"Having lots of ideas is a good thing, but you should listen to your friends too," Pat explained.

"I suppose so," said Sarah.

"I am sure they are missing you, why not try and be friends again?"

Sarah thought for a moment, "OK," she said.

"Good girl, and whilst you are on your way, could you look out for Jess, I haven't seen him since this morning," said Pat.

Pat was right, the other children did miss Sarah.

"It's not the same without Sarah," said Meera. "I think we should find her and say sorry."

The others agreed, and off they set, bumping into Alf on their way.

"Want a lift children?" he asked.

"YES, please!" they all chorused.

Meanwhile, Ted was flying around with his litter blower.

"Are you alright Ted?" asked PC Selby.

"Aye!" said Ted.

Just then, Sarah walked by looking for Jess. Have you seen Jess?" she asked. Both PC Selby and Ted shook their heads and continued to blow the litter into piles.

Suddenly, a piece of litter blew up into the air and it stuck in the branch of a tree. All of a sudden, Jess ran across the green after it, and straight up the tree.

"Meow …" Jess chirped, as he teetered on the branch.

"Oh, careful Jess!" gasped Sarah, but it was no good, he was stuck up the tree.

Sarah ran to the Station Café, "Help!" she cried as she burst through the door. "What is the matter, Sarah?" Ajay asked. "Jess is stuck up a tree!" said Sarah. Ajay and Nisha fetched a ladder.

When they got back to the tree, Jess was still perched on the branch. "Meow!" he whimpered. "Stand back, Sarah!" said Ajay, but he was frightening Jess. Soon Pat arrived, "JESS!" he said, sounding alarmed. "PAT!" Sarah cried. Jess was trembling on the branch.

Meanwhile, the tractor pulled up, and the other children saw Sarah, Nisha, Ajay and Pat standing by the tree.

"What's Sarah doing?" said Meera. The children ran towards the tree.

"Oh, hello, I thought you were playing spaceships," said Sarah.

"We are sorry about what happened and we would like you to be our Mission Commander again!" said Bill

"But what's going on here?" asked Julian. Sarah explained to the others about Jess getting stuck.

PC Selby and Ted were still blowing litter, when they reached the tree and saw Jess trembling on the branch.

"Alright! Nobody panic!" said PC Selby.

Hearing the commotion, Mrs Goggins arrived with a blanket. "I've got a blanket, we can hold the corners, and Jess can jump down into it!"

But Jess was scared, and leapt on to a higher branch.

"Oh, no!" said Pat. "How will we get Jess down?"

Suddenly, there was a whooshing sound.

"What is that?" asked Pat.

"It's Ted's Litter Blower!" said PC Selby, as everyone watched Ted hover around.

"Pat! I've got an idea!" Sarah said excitedly, "we could use Ted's machine to fly up and get Jess down!"

Everyone thought it was great idea.

"You're Mission Commander Sarah!" Julian said.

"OK, hold on Jess, I'm coming!" said Sarah. Ted showed her how to operate the Litter Blower, and everyone counted her down, "FIVE, FOUR, THREE, TWO, ONE

...blast off!" Sarah reached up to the branch and lifted Jess down.

"Hurray!" cried Bill as Jess and Sarah landed safely on the ground.

"Well done Sarah!"

everyone shouted together.

Postman Pat's Christmas Eve

It was Christmas Eve in Greendale, and the village was covered in a soft, snowy blanket.

The Post Office was full of mail sacks.

"What a lot of post!" said Pat. "I hope I get it delivered in time! It's the Christmas show tonight and I don't want to miss it. Meera is Cinderella and Julian is Prince Charming!"

"Meow!" said Jess.

"Oh yes, I nearly forgot," said Pat. "Jess is Cinderella's cat and Pumpkin's going to pull the coach."

Pat took the post to the village hall. It was very noisy there!

"It's the last rehearsal before the show," said Jeff.

"But everyone's being silly," said Meera.

Just then Bill swooped in on his skateboard. "Ugly sister coming through!" he said, and Jess leapt into the air and bumped into the scenery.

"Meow!" said Jess.

"This is awful!" cried Meera.

"No one's taking it seriously!"

Ajay had set off extra early to collect the village Christmas tree from Pencaster. But the snow was very thick, and the Rocket was still a long way from Greendale.

Ajay stopped at the Halt to fill the Rocket's boiler with water, but the water was frozen! "I hope we've got enough to get us home," he said.

When Pat had delivered all the post, he went to the station to help Ajay with the tree. But he still hadn't arrived, and Nisha was worried.

"I'll find him," said Pat.

Out in the countryside, the Rocket was still chugging along ... until a snowdrift blocked the line. "I've got some digging to do," said Ajay. But he had forgotten the shovel.

The Rocket was stuck in the snow!

Pat drove up a steep lane, looking for Ajay. But the van's wheels spun in the snow. Then it skidded and stopped.

"What do I do now?" said Pat.

Then he had an idea!

Pat steered the van backwards down the hill into the village.

"Can I borrow Pumpkin, Amy?" said Pat. "I need to find Ajay and the Rocket. Pumpkin can go where my van can't."

Just then, Ted arrived with the sleigh that was going to be Cinderella's coach.

"That's just what I need!" said Pat, and soon Pumpkin was trotting through the snow pulling Pat in the sleigh.

When Pat found Ajay, they put the tree on the sleigh and set off back to Greendale. Clever Pumpkin knew the way, even in the snow!

They got back in time to hear the audience cheering and clapping at the end of the show.

"Well done, Meera!" said Ajay. "Now come outside, everyone. There's a special surprise on the village green!"

It was the Christmas tree!

"Wow!" said Meera. "You and Pat even put presents under the tree, Dad!"

Just then, they heard the tinkle of sleigh bells and a jolly laugh.

Pat smiled. "We didn't bring the presents," he said. "But I think I know who did! Do you?

Merry Christmas, everyone!"

The End